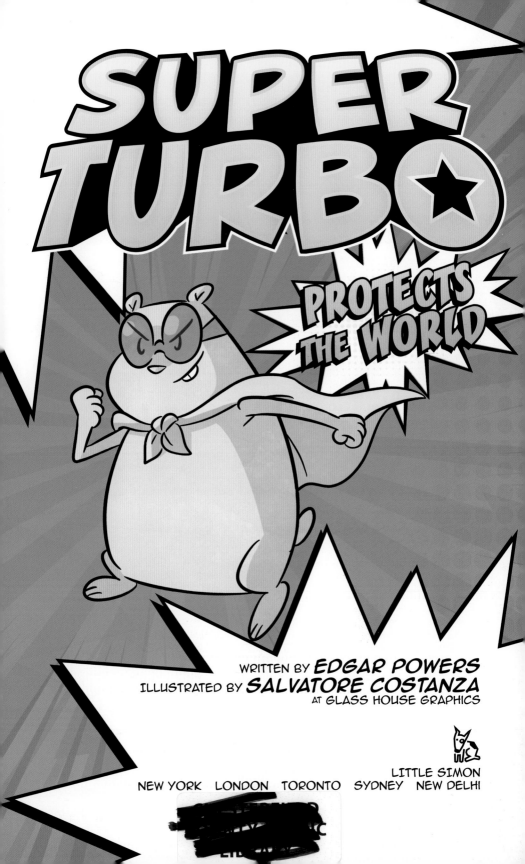

SUPER TURBO ★

PROTECTS THE WORLD

WRITTEN BY **EDGAR POWERS**
ILLUSTRATED BY **SALVATORE COSTANZA**
AT GLASS HOUSE GRAPHICS

LITTLE SIMON
NEW YORK   LONDON   TORONTO   SYDNEY   NEW DELHI

LITTLE SIMON

AN IMPRINT OF SIMON & SCHUSTER CHILDREN'S PUBLISHING DIVISION 1230 AVENUE OF THE AMERICAS, NEW YORK, NEW YORK 10020 FIRST LITTLE SIMON EDITION AUGUST 2021 * COPYRIGHT © 2021 BY SIMON & SCHUSTER, INC. ALL RIGHTS RESERVED, INCLUDING THE RIGHT OF REPRODUCTION IN WHOLE OR IN PART IN ANY FORM. LITTLE SIMON IS A REGISTERED TRADEMARK OF SIMON & SCHUSTER, INC., AND ASSOCIATED COLOPHON IS A TRADEMARK OF SIMON & SCHUSTER, INC. FOR INFORMATION ABOUT SPECIAL DISCOUNTS FOR BULK PURCHASES, PLEASE CONTACT SIMON & SCHUSTER SPECIAL SALES AT 1-866-506-1949 OR BUSINESS@SIMONANDSCHUSTER.COM. THE SIMON & SCHUSTER SPEAKERS BUREAU CAN BRING AUTHORS TO YOUR LIVE EVENT. FOR MORE INFORMATION OR TO BOOK AN EVENT CONTACT THE SIMON & SCHUSTER SPEAKERS BUREAU AT 1-866-248-3049 OR VISIT OUR WEBSITE AT WWW.SIMONSPEAKERS.COM. DESIGNED BY NICHOLAS SCIACCA * ART SERVICES BY GLASS HOUSE GRAPHICS * ART AND COLOR BY SALVATORE COSTANZA * LETTERING BY GIOVANNI SPATARO/GRAFIMATED CARTOON * SUPERVISION BY SALVATORE DI MARCO/GRAFIMATED CARTOON * MANUFACTURED IN CHINA 0521 SCP * 2 4 6 8 10 9 7 5 3 1 * LIBRARY OF CONGRESS CATALOGING-IN-PUBLICATION DATA NAMES: POWERS, EDGAR J., AUTHOR. | GLASS HOUSE GRAPHICS, ILLUSTRATOR. TITLE: SUPER TURBO PROTECTS THE WORLD / BY EDGAR J. POWERS ; ILLUSTRATED BY GLASS HOUSE GRAPHICS. DESCRIPTION: FIRST LITTLE SIMON EDITION. | NEW YORK : LITTLE SIMON, 2021. | SERIES: SUPER TURBO, THE GRAPHIC NOVEL ; BOOK 4 | AUDIENCE: AGES 5-9 | AUDIENCE: GRADES K-4 | SUMMARY: DURING CELEBRATE-THE-WORLD DAY AT SUNNYVIEW ELEMENTARY SUPER TURBO AND THE OTHER SUPERPETS PROTECT THE SCHOOL AND THE WORLD FROM WHISKERFACE. IDENTIFIERS: LCCN 2020027937 (PRINT) | LCCN 2020027938 (EBOOK) | ISBN 9781534478411 (PAPERBACK) | ISBN 9781534478428 (HARDCOVER) | ISBN 9781534478435 (EBOOK) SUBJECTS: LCSH: GRAPHIC NOVELS. | CYAC: GRAPHIC NOVELS. | SUPERHEROES—FICTION. | HAMSTERS—FICTION. | PETS—FICTION. | ELEMENTARY SCHOOLS—FICTION. | SCHOOLS—FICTION. CLASSIFICATION: LCC PZ7.7.P7 SN 2021 (PRINT) | LCC PZ7.7.P7 (EBOOK) | DDC 741.5/973—DC23 LC RECORD AVAILABLE AT HTTPS://LCCN.LOC.GOV/2020027937 LC EBOOK RECORD AVAILABLE AT HTTPS://LCCN.LOC.GOV/2020027938

CONTENTS

TURBO LOOKED AROUND. NOW HE REMEMBERED!

BEING A *GECKO*, LEO LIVED IN A TERRARIUM, WHERE IT WAS HOT!

TURBO LIVED IN A *COZY CAGE* IN CLASSROOM C. IT HAD A BED, WOOD CHIPS, AND A HAMSTER WHEEL.

IT WAS VERY DIFFERENT FROM A TERRARIUM.

AND WAY LESS HOT!

TURBO AND LEO ARE OFFICIAL CLASSROOM PETS (AND SECRET SUPERHEROES) AT SUNNYVIEW ELEMENTARY.

Sunnyview Elementary

THEY ARE NOT THE ONLY CLASSROOM PETS...OR SECRET SUPERHEROES!

SUNNYVIEW ELEMENTARY IS PROTECTED BY A SECRET *GROUP* OF SUPERHERO CLASSROOM PETS.

BUT MORE ON THAT LATER!

MAYBE WE SHOULD GET YOU SOMETHING TO DRINK.

AAAAAHH!

13

TAP! TAP! TAP!

DID YOU *HEAR* THAT?

IT'S THE SUPERPET SUPERHERO LEAGUE *ALARM!*

THREE TAPS MEANS IT'S AN *EMERGENCY!*

SUPER TURBO AND THE GREAT GECKO QUICKLY REMOVED THE VENT COVER FROM THE VENT IN CLASSROOM A AND ENTERED THE VENT SYSTEM.

THE VENT SYSTEM CONNECTED ALL THE CLASSROOMS, AND IT WAS HOW THE SUPERPETS TRAVELED *FROM ROOM TO ROOM.*

INSIDE THE VENT, TURBO AND LEO LISTENED CLOSELY TO THE SOUND OF THE TAPS.

TAP! TAP! TAP!

SOFT, WITH A LITTLE BOUNCE ON THE END.

A PENCIL ERASER!

CLEVER IS CALLING US!

CLEVER WAS A PARAKEET AND THE OFFICIAL CLASSROOM PET OF CLASSROOM D.

SHE WAS ALSO A MEMBER OF THE SUPERPET SUPERHERO LEAGUE, WHERE SHE FOUGHT EVIL AS THE *GREEN WINGER*.

EACH PET USED A DIFFERENT TOOL TO TAP FOR HELP. CLEVER USED A *PENCIL ERASER.*

TURBO'S TOOL WAS A *RULER.*

LEO'S WAS A *CRAYON.*

EVERY SUPERPET KNEW THAT THREE TAPS MEANT AN *EMERGENCY.* THE DIFFERENT SOUNDS CREATE BY THE DIFFERENT TOOLS LET THE OTHER PETS KNOW WHO NEEDED HELP.

TAP! TAP! TAP!

NOW YOU KNOW OUR TOP SECRET COMMUNICATION SYSTEM. JUST MAKE SURE NOT TO TELL ANYONE!

TURBO AND LEO RAN THROUGH THE VENTS TOWARD CLASSROOM D.

AS THEY ROUNDED A CORNER, THEY BUMPED INTO THE OTHER MEMBERS OF THE SUPERPET SUPERHERO LEAGUE.

THEY ARE...

ANGELINA, ALSO KNOWN AS *WONDER PIG*, FROM CLASSROOM B. SHE'S A GUINEA PIG, AND SHE'S REALLY GOOD AT MAZES.

I'M ALSO SUPERSTRONG!

FRANK, ALSO KNOWN AS *BOSS BUNNY*, LIVES IN THE PRINCIPAL'S OFFICE. HIS UTILITY BELT HAS A GADGET FOR ANY OCCASION!

I CAN ALSO SMELL DANGER!

WARREN, WHOSE SUPERHERO ALIAS IS *PROFESSOR TURTLE*, LIVES IN THE SCIENCE LAB. BEING A TURTLE, HE'S PRETTY SLOW. BUT HE'S SUPERSMART!

ESPECIALLY... WHEN IT COMES... TO SCIENCE!

WONDER PIG USED HER SUPERSTRENGTH TO REMOVE THE VENT COVER FROM CLASSROOM D.

THANK GOODNESS YOU'RE HERE! COME QUICK!

IT'S NELL, ALSO KNOWN AS *FANTASTIC FISH.*

SHE LIVES IN AN AQUARIUM IN THE HALL. BECAUSE SHE MUST STAY IN WATER, SHE TRAVELS IN THE WATER-FILLED TURBOMOBILE.

THE TURBOMOBILE SPRANG A *LEAK!*

I CAN'T GET HER BACK TO HER AQUARIUM BY MYSELF!

SUPERPETS, LET'S *DO* THIS!

SO THEY DID *THIS.*

AND *THIS.*

AND *THIS.*

AND OF COURSE *THIS.*

THEN THEY DID *THIS.*

AND *THIS.*

UNTIL FINALLY...

SUDDENLY ALL THE SUPERPETS REALIZED HOW *TIRED* THEY WERE.

CHAPTER 3

TURBO SLEPT SOUNDLY AND WOKE UP THE NEXT MORNING JUST AS THE *BELL* WAS RINGING.

TURBO!
Official Classroom Pet
CLASSROOM C

RING-A-DING-DING!

A NEW SCHOOL DAY HAD BEGUN, AND THE STUDENTS WERE FILING INTO CLASSROOM C.

REMEMBER HOW WE TOLD YOU THAT TURBO IS A *SECRET* SUPERHERO?

WELL, THAT MEANS HE HAS TO ACT LIKE AN *ORDINARY* HAMSTER IN FRONT OF THE STUDENTS AND MS. BEASLEY.

RUNNING ON HIS WHEEL...

HUFF! PUFF!

...MUNCHING ON HIS PELLETS...

CRUNCH! MUNCH!

...AND DRINKING FROM HIS WATER BOTTLE.

GLUG!

GLUG!

JUST THEN, TURBO NOTICED THAT MS. BEASLEY WAS ABOUT TO MAKE AN ANNOUNCEMENT.

I HAVE SOME EXCITING *NEWS!*

FOR THE NEXT SEVERAL DAYS, THE WHOLE SCHOOL IS PARTICIPATING IN A *SPECIAL PROJECT.*

Cele... the W... Day...

TURBO'S EARS PERKED UP. A SPECIAL PROJECT SOUNDED LIKE IMPORTANT SUPERHERO BUSINESS.

THE SPECIAL PROJECT IS...

...CELEBRATE THE WORLD DAY!

WHAT'S CELEBRATE THE WORLD DAY?

WE'LL LEARN ALL ABOUT DIFFERENT COUNTRIES! ISN'T THAT *EXCITING?*

EVERYONE WAS EXCITED ABOUT CELEBRATE THE WORLD DAY— ESPECIALLY TURBO!

MS. BEASLEY ANNOUNCED WHICH COUNTRY EACH DIFFERENT CLASSROOM WOULD BE CELEBRATING.

CLASSROOM A WAS *BRAZIL.*

CLASSROOM B WAS *ITALY.*

CLASSROOM D WAS *KENYA.*

THE SCIENCE LAB WAS **SWITZERLAND.**

THE HALLWAYS WERE **CHINA.**

PRINCIPAL BRICKFORD'S OFFICE WAS **RUSSIA.**

AND CLASSROOM C WAS...

CHAPTER 4

THAT EVENING THE SUPERPET SUPERHERO LEAGUE HELD THEIR MEETING IN THE HALLWAY SO NELL COULD ATTEND.

HOW ARE **THE REPAIRS** ON THE TURBOMOBILE COMING ALONG, PROFESSOR TURTLE?

BEFORE THE MEETING, THE SUPERPETS HAD GATHERED BOOKS FROM THE LIBRARY SO THEY COULD *LEARN* ABOUT THEIR COUNTRIES.

IT SAYS HERE THAT JAPAN IS MADE UP OF *6,852* SEPARATE *ISLANDS.* THAT'S PRETTY COOL!

ALMOST AS COOL AS THE FACT THAT KENYA HAS *ELEPHANTS!*

GUYS, I DON'T WANT TO BRAG, BUT DID YOU KNOW THAT BRAZIL IS THE *BIGGEST COUNTRY* IN SOUTH AMERICA?

BIG DEAL! RUSSIA IS THE BIGGEST COUNTRY IN THE *WHOLE WORLD!*

BUT CHINA HAS THE LARGEST *POPULATION!*

RHINOCEROSES LIVE IN KENYA! THAT'S WAY MORE EXCITING!

WHILE THE SUPERPETS WERE BUSY DOING THIS, THEY DIDN'T NOTICE SOMETHING IMPORTANT...

THEY WERE BEING SPIED ON BY TWO *RAT PACKERS!*

THE SUPERPETS ALSO MISSED *THIS*...

...AND *THIS*...

...WHICH MEANS THEY HAVE NO IDEA *THIS* WAS HAPPENING.

THE KINDERGARTEN STUDENTS IN CLASSROOM A WILL BE CELEBRATING BRAZIL.

THE MOST POPULAR SPORT IN BRAZIL IS *SOCCER*.

THEY CALL IT *FUTEBOL*.

IT MEANS THE SAME THING!

BUT YOU SAID IT *WRONG!*

ENOUGH! JUST TELL ME WHAT THEY ARE PLANNING AND HOW WE WILL RUIN IT!

THEY'RE PLANNING TO BUILD A *MINIATURE FUTEBOL STADIUM*, BUT WE'LL DESTROY IT!

CHAPTER 5

THE NEXT DAY, THE STUDENTS OF SUNNYVIEW WORKED HARD TO DECORATE THEIR CLASSROOMS.

ALL THE EXCITEMENT IN CLASSROOM C HAD TIRED TURBO OUT...

TURBO!
Official Classroom Pet
CLASSROOM C

...AND HE WAS
FAST ASLEEP.
UNTIL...

SQUEAK!

DID YOU HEAR THAT?

SQUEAK!

HELLO? IS ANYONE THERE?

THE SQUEAKING STOPPED! THAT'S *SUSPICIOUS!*

YOU CAN TAKE OVER FOR NOW, NARRATOR. JUST MAKE SURE TO *WHISPER!*

USING HIS SUPER-HAMSTER AGILITY, TURBO SNUCK OUT OF HIS CAGE...

...AND SCAMPERED ACROSS THE CLASSROOM, TOWARD MS. BEASLEY'S DESK, WHERE THE SQUEAKING SOUND HAD BEEN COMING FROM.

THAT'S WHEN HE DISCOVERED THAT THE BOTTOM DRAWER WAS *OPEN!*

TURBO TOOK A FEW STEPS BACK AND REALIZED THAT ALL THE DRAWERS WERE OPEN, THOUGH THE TOP TWO DRAWERS WERE ONLY OPEN PARTWAY.

IT LOOKS LIKE A *STAIRCASE.*

I'M NOT SURE WHAT TURBO IS THINKING, BECAUSE I'M NOT A MIND READER, BUT...

I WAS THINKING IT LOOKS LIKE A STAIRCASE...AND I'M GONNA CLIMB THAT STAIRCASE!

DISPLAYING A SPEED SELDOM SEEN IN HAMSTERS, SUPER TURBO RACED TOWARD THE STAIRCASE DRAWERS...

OUCH!

WHOOPS. EVEN WITH HIS SUPER-HAMSTER SPEED, SUPER TURBO WAS TOO SMALL TO MAKE IT ONTO THE FIRST STEP.

SUPER TURBO NEEDED A BOOST.

LOOK AT HIM GO!

HE DID IT!

THE WOOD-AND-PAPER **SHOJI WALLS** BY THE CUBBIES.

THE **JAPANESE GARDEN** BY THE WINDOWS.

THE **TEA SET** BY THE READING NOOK.

THE MODEL OF **MOUNT FUJI** OVER BY THAT CRACK IN THE WALL.

AS TURBO LOOKED AT ALL THE WONDERFUL DECORATIONS, HE REALIZED SOMETHING.

THE STUDENTS OF CLASSROOM C HAD WORKED REALLY, REALLY HARD.

NOW MORE THAN EVER, HE NEEDED TO KEEP A WATCHFUL EYE OVER HIS CLASSROOM.

JUST THEN, TURBO HEARD ANOTHER SOUND. BUT THIS TIME IT WAS TAPPING.

TAP! TAP! TAP!

IT WAS THE *SUPERPET SUPERHERO ALARM!*

ALL THE SUPERPETS QUICKLY ANSWERED THE GREAT GECKO'S DISTRESS CALL, EXCEPT FOR FANTASTIC FISH, WHO WAS STUCK IN HER TANK.

WHAT'S THE EMERGENCY HERE, GREAT GECKO?

LOOK AT THIS BANNER! IT'S *RUINED!*

I'LL SAY! IT LOOKS LIKE IT WAS PAINTED BY A BUNCH OF FIVE-YEAR-OLDS!

THAT'S BECAUSE IT *WAS* PAINTED BY A BUNCH OF FIVE-YEAR-OLDS! THE KIDS IN MY CLASS MADE IT!

THEY MADE IT TO CELEBRATE CLASSROOM A'S COUNTRY, BRAZIL. THEY WORKED REALLY HARD ON IT!

AND NOW IT'S DESTROYED.

WHAT DO YOU THINK HAPPENED TO IT?

I WAS ASLEEP IN MY TERRARIUM WHEN I HEARD SOME NOISES.

FIRST I HEARD A *SQUEAKING* SOUND, AND THEN A RIPPING SOUND, LIKE PAPER WAS BEING TORN.

I INVESTIGATED AND I FOUND... THIS.

SQUEAKING, YOU SAY?

WHAT ARE YOU THINKING, SUPER TURBO?

I'M BEGINNING TO SMELL A *RAT!* MAKE THAT, A MOUSE WHO LIKES TO THINK HE'S A RAT, NAMED...

...WHISKERFACE!

THIS DEFINITELY SMELLS LIKE THE WORK OF WHISKERFACE AND HIS RAT PACK! AND IF THEY ARE OUT THERE SOMEWHERE...

...AND WE ARE ALL IN HERE...

MY CLASSROOM IS CLOSEST! LET'S ALL HEAD TO CLASSROOM B!

OH NO!

THE LEANING TOWER OF PISA ISN'T SUPPOSED TO BE LEANING *THAT MUCH!*

JUST THEN, TURBO HEARD NELL CALLING OUT FROM THE HALLWAY.

SUPERPETS! I JUST SAW THEM! THEY RAN UNDER THE DOOR INTO THE PRINCIPAL'S OFFICE!

NO ONE MESSES WITH PRINCIPAL BRICKFORD'S OFFICE!

THEY'RE GETTING AWAY! HURRY, SUPERPETS!

THE SUPERPETS WORKED ALL NIGHT TO PUT THEIR CLASSROOMS AND THE SCIENCE LAB BACK IN ORDER.

AFTER EVERYTHING WAS *CLEANED UP*, THE SUPERPETS SPENT THE NEXT FEW DAYS CAREFULLY PATROLLING THE SCHOOL.

THEY WERE LOOKING FOR ANY SIGN OF MISCHIEF FROM THE RAT PACK...

BUT NOTHING HAPPENED.

WHICH BRINGS US BACK TO TODAY— *CELEBRATE THE WORLD DAY!*

SOON IT WOULD BE TIME FOR THE GREAT FEAST IN THE CAFETERIA TO BEGIN!

THERE WOULD BE FOODS FROM AROUND THE WORLD! FOOD LIKE...

SUSHI.

RICE AND BEANS.

PIZZA.

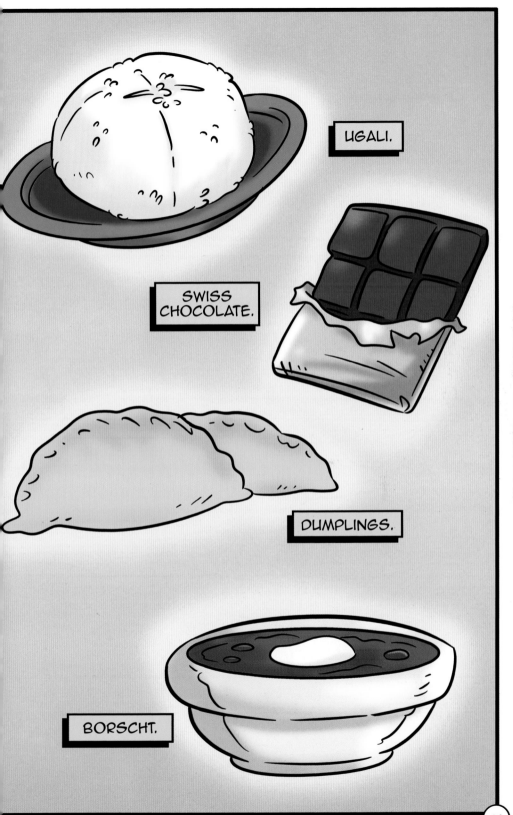

UGALI.

SWISS CHOCOLATE.

DUMPLINGS.

BORSCHT.

TURBO THOUGHT ALL THE FOODS THAT WOULD BE AT THE FEAST SOUNDED *DELICIOUS*...

...EXCEPT FOR MAYBE THE *BORSCHT*. THAT REALLY DID SOUND GROSS.

BUT HE COULDN'T LET THE THOUGHTS OF THE FEAST DISTRACT HIM.

THERE WAS IMPORTANT SUPERHERO BUSINESS TO ATTEND TO!

AS SOON AS EVERYONE LEFT FOR THE FEAST, THE SUPERPET SUPERHERO LEAGUE WAS GOING TO HAVE AN EMERGENCY MEETING.

IT WAS TIME FOR THE FEAST TO BEGIN!

RING-A-DING-DING

THE STUDENTS RUSHED OFF TO THE CAFETERIA.

TURBO RUSHED OFF TO HIS MEETING.

THE SUPERPETS KNEW THAT IF THE RAT PACK WAS GOING TO STRIKE, IT WOULD HAPPEN TODAY.

THAT'S WHY THEY WERE HAVING AN EMERGENCY MEETING.

I...LOVE... DRESSING... UP.

ME TOO!

EVERYONE LOOKS *GREAT!*

BUT WHERE'S BOSS BUNNY?

ANY SIGN OF WHISKERFACE?

NOW THAT THE WHOLE SCHOOL IS IN THE CAFETERIA, MY RAT PACK IS GOING TO *LOCK* THEM IN THERE!

NO, YOU'RE NOT! WE'LL *STOP* YOU!

NO, YOU WON'T, GREAT *GEEK-O!*

YES, WE WILL!

OH NO, YOU WON'T, SUPER *TURD-O!*

RIGHT NOW, I HAVE AGENTS IN EVERY ONE OF YOUR CLASSROOMS.

ONCE I GIVE MY SIGNAL, THE REST OF MY *RAT PACK* WILL JOIN THEM.

THEY'LL LEAP INTO ACTION AND *DESTROY* EVERYTHING! EVERY CLASSROOM PROJECT!

HAHAHAHAHAHA!

SNAP

THAT WAS THE SIGNAL!

SUDDENLY THE RAT PACKERS BEGAN TO SWARM THE HALLWAY.

THEY CAME FROM EVERY DIRECTION...

...A SEEMINGLY ENDLESS ARMY.

HOW MANY OF THEM ARE THERE?

UM....SO MANY!

JUST WHEN IT LOOKED LIKE THE SUPERPETS MIGHT BE DEFEATED...

RUMBLE! RUMBLE!

RUMBLE! RUMBLE!

WHAT'S THAT SOUND?

SORRY WE'RE LATE!

ACTUALLY, I'D SAY YOU'RE RIGHT ON TIME!

GO, FANTASTIC FISH!

KNOCK 'EM DOWN!

WHAT IS HAPPENING?!

BUT FANTASTIC FISH KNEW EXACTLY WHAT SHE WAS DOING.

AT THE LAST SECOND, SHE UNLATCHED THE TOP OF THE FANTASTIC FISH TANK...

...AND *LEAPED OUT*, JUST IN THE NICK OF TIME!

WHICH MADE *THIS* HAPPEN...

RETREAT!

NELL!

NOT AGAIN!

GET BACK IN YOUR CLASSROOMS!

SUPER TURBO, HIDE THE FANTASTIC FISH TANK!

OH! I RENAMED THE TURBOMOBILE! I HOPE THAT'S OKAY!

OF COURSE IT IS! BUT WE CAN'T *LEAVE* YOU HERE!

I'LL BE FINE! WITH THE COMMOTION WE CREATED, PEOPLE ARE GOING TO COME RUNNING!

ANY SECOND NOW SOMEONE WILL HELP ME!

THAT'S WHAT I CALL A *HERO!*

137

THE STUDENTS OF SUNNYVIEW HAVE NO IDEA HOW CLOSE CELEBRATE THE WORLD DAY CAME TO BEING RUINED.

I'M SURE WE HAVEN'T SEEN THE LAST OF WHISKERFACE...

NO, BUT WE'LL BE READY FOR HIM!

THE SUPERPET
SUPERHERO LEAGUE WILL
ALWAYS BE READY WHEN THE
SCHOOL—AND THE WORLD—
NEED PROTECTING!

CAN'T GET ENOUGH OF THE **SUPERPET SUPERHERO LEAGUE?** CHECK OUT THEIR NEXT ADVENTURE...

TURN THE PAGE FOR A SNEAK PEEK...